The PETAL PALS
Beat the Heat

by Denise Coughlin & Maria Pappas

Illustrated by Thomson Digital

To my husband, thank you for your patience and understanding pertaining to all the outrageous adventures Maria and I try.

To my children, may *The Petal Pals* bring you as much joy as you have brought to me. Always have the courage to follow your dreams and never accept "No" for an answer.

To my parents, I am extremely grateful for your never ending love and support. The confidence that you have instilled in me and your generosity has made this book possible.

To my co-author and partner in crime, I especially thank you from the bottom of my heart for helping me make this idea a reality. You truly are my best friend.

– I love you all, Denise

To my husband, Jonathan-My life would not be the same without your never ending love, patience, and sense of humor. Thank you for being by my side through all of life's twists and turns.

To my parents-You are always in my heart. Not a day goes by that you are not in my thoughts.

To my Nouno-Words cannot fully express how I feel about you. You mean the world to me.

To my special 'family of friends'-You enrich my life everyday by being in it.

To Denise- Your friendship is a treasure that I will always hold close to my heart. Thank you for including me in your dream of bringing *The Petal Pals* to life. I couldn't have asked for a better best friend.

– I love you all, Maria

To Nick, thank you for believing in *The Petal Pals*. Your guidance throughout this entire process has been invaluable. Finally to our pals, the 'Girls Night Out Crew', your friendship means the world to us.

– Denise & Maria

Copyright © 2008 Denise Coughlin and Maria Pappas

NK Publications
PO Box 1735
Radio City Station
New York, NY 10101
www.nkpublications.com

"The Petal Pals" have been registered with the U.S. Trademark office

Just over the hill, at the end of Blossom
Lane, is the Denmar flower shop.
It has the most beautiful gardens in
all of Sunnyville.

Living in these colorful gardens is a special group of friends. Their names are Rose, Violet, Daisy and Lily, but they like to call themselves the Petal Pals.

Meet Rose and Violet. Rose thinks she is the prettiest flower of the garden. She likes to smell nice and enjoys playing dress up. Violet is the sporty one of the group. She loves to play games and sometimes gets in trouble.

"Hey Violet, do you want to paint your leaf tips with me?" asked Rose.

"No thanks. I'm playing hopscotch. Why don't you ask Daisy?" answered Violet.

Say hello to Daisy and Lily. Daisy
is very smart. She enjoys reading
books and going to school. Lily
is the most caring flower in the
garden. She likes to help others and
always follows the rules.

"Lily, did
you know that
we need both water and
sunlight to grow?" asked Daisy.

"I didn't know that. I'm glad you are always
teaching me new things," said Lily.

One Sunday afternoon the Petal
Pals were having fun jumping
rope. After jumping for a long
time in the hot sun, they needed to
cool off.

"I am so thirsty! My petals are wilting and
I look terrible!" whined Rose.

"Why don't we go swimming in the pond?"
suggested Violet.

"We are not allowed to go in the pond. It
is too deep and dangerous," said Lily.

"Then let's run through the sprinkler,"
replied Daisy.

The Petal Pals ran to the house to play in the sprinkler. But the hose was too heavy to move and the spout to turn on the water was stuck. Violet, Daisy, and Lily each tried their hardest lifting the hose and turning the spout but it would not budge.

"Don't look at me," said Rose. "I'm not going to try lifting that heavy hose. I just painted my tips this beautiful shade of pink!"

Just then a very unusual bumblebee appeared.

"Bling is my name and singing is my game. I am cool, witty and from the city," he sang.

"Get out of here!" screeched Rose. I can't stand bugs."

"Rose, that's not very nice. Besides, he may be able to help," said Lily.

Bling smiled at Lily and said, "If you want to get cool, what you need are some tools."

"That's it!" shouted Daisy. "Bling, you have given me a great idea! If we all work together, we can move the hose and turn on the water."

The Petal Pals and Bling listened carefully as Daisy explained her plan.

Afterwards, everyone knew exactly what they had to do.

"Don't worry about your troubles, I'll be back on the double," sang Bling as he flew away.

Meanwhile, Violet, Daisy, and Lily worked together to uncurl the hose. Then, Rose attached the sprinkler very carefully without chipping any of her leaf tips.

Iris was knitting and watching all of this from the shade of the back porch when Bling flew up to her and asked, "Excuse me ma'am, you sure are looking fine, may the Petal Pals borrow some of your twine?"

"I suppose so", replied Iris. "But please be careful and return it so I can finish my knitting."

Bling thanked her and took the yarn back to his new friends.

When Bling returned with the yarn, he and the Petal Pals wrapped it around the spout. Next, all of them pulled and pulled the yarn with all their might. Just when they were about to give up, the water began shooting out of the sprinkler like giant raindrops.

"Hooray, we did it!" yelled Violet.

The Petal Pals had a great time running
through the sprinkler. The cold water felt so
good as it splashed down upon them. They
had beaten the heat!

After a while, Bling had to go home. "Looks
like it's time for me to flee. My fellow bees
are missing me. I'll be back, you can count on
that," he sang buzzing away.

As the sun began to set, the Petal Pals were all tired from their busy day. They had so much fun and learned that anything is possible with a little help from their friends.

"I can't wait for tomorrow. The flower shop is having a sale. I hope we go some place fabulous like a birthday party," exclaimed Violet as she let out a great big yawn.

About the authors

Denise Coughlin and Maria Pappas first crossed each others paths, literally, as they were walking to school on their first day of kindergarten. The two of them have been best friends ever since.

Denise Coughlin is a graduate of Michigan State University and a former Certified Public Accountant. She resides in Brighton, Michigan with her husband where they enjoy raising their three children. Her oldest daughter's passion for reading inspired Denise to create The Petal Pals. As she treasures her childhood memories of the simple times spent with her friends, she hopes that these characters and their adventures capture that same innocence.

Maria Pappas received her Bachelor's and Master's degrees in Elementary Education from Wayne State University. Currently, she is pursuing a Master's Degree in School Counseling. For the past 17 years she has taught elementary and middle school children in the Detroit Public Schools. She is happily married and lives with her husband in Grosse Pointe Woods, Michigan. Sharing special moments with her friends is something she cherishes.

Imagine all the exciting places The Petal Pals will go to and all the fun they will have growing up. Don't miss your chance to be a part of their lives! Be on the look out for more of their adventures coming soon.

For now, you can visit Rose, Violet, Daisy, and Lily at www.thepetalpals.com